TO MY SWEET JACOB, AND ALL THE CATS
HE'S EVER KNOWN, ESPECIALLY MAX
—K.A.

TO COLIN AND VEDA
FOR ALWAYS BEING HAPPY TO PLAY
—P.D.

ATHENEUM BOOKS FOR YOUNG READERS • An imprint of Simon & Schuster Children's Publishing Division •1230 Avenue of the Americas, New York, New York 10020 • Text copyright © 2019 by Kathi Appelt • Illustrations copyright © 2019 by Penelope Dullaghan • All rights reserved, including the right of reproduction in whole or in part in any form. • ATHENEUM BOOKS FOR YOUNG READERS is a registered trademark of Simon & Schuster, Inc. • Atheneum logo is a trademark of Simon & Schuster, Inc. • For information about special discounts for bulk purchases, please contact Simon & Schuster Special Sales at 1-866-506-1949 or business@simonandschuster.com. • The Simon & Schuster Speakers Bureau can bring authors to your live event. For more information or to book an event, • contact the Simon & Schuster Speakers Bureau at 1-866-248-3049 or visit our website at www.simonspeakers.com. • Book design by Sonia Chaghatzbanian • The text for this book was set in Brush Up. • The illustrations for this book are rendered in acrylic, charcoal, and digital • Manufactured in China • 0319 SCP • First Edition • 10 9 8 7 6 5 4 3 2 1 • Library of Congress Cataloging-in-Publication Data • Names: Appelt, Kathi, 1954- author. | Dullaghan, Penelope, illustrator. • Title: Max attacks / Kathi Appelt ; illustrated by Penelope Dullaghan. • Description: New York : Atheneum Books for Young Readers, 2019. | "A Caitlyn Dlouhy book." | Summary: Max the cat attacks fish, curtains, socks, and strings, but how many things can he actually catch? • Identifiers: LCCN 2018045166| ISBN 9781481451468 (hardback) | ISBN 9781481451475 (eBook) • Subjects: | CYAC: Stories in rhyme. | Cats—Fiction. | Humorous stories. | BISAC: JUVENILE FICTION / Animals / Cats. | JUVENILE FICTION / Humorous Stories. | JUVENILE FICTION / Action & Adventure / General. • Classification: LCC PZ8.3.A554 Max 2019 | DDC [E]—dc23 LC record available at https://lccn.loc.gov/2018045166

Max ATTACKS

KATHI APPELT

PICTURES BY
PENELOPE DULLAGHAN

A CAITLYN DLOUHY BOOK
Atheneum ATHENEUM BOOKS FOR YOUNG READERS
NEW YORK LONDON TORONTO SYDNEY NEW DELHI

THIS IS Max. HE ATTACKS.

IN A BOWL OF WATER BRIMMING . . .

FISHES!

LOTS OF FISHES SWIMMING.

MAX'S PAWS ARE MADE FOR POUNCES.
MAX'S LEGS ARE BUILT FOR TROUNCES.

LIKE A DOZEN KITTY WISHES, MIDST THE BUBBLES SWISH THE FISHES.

BUT
HOLD ON . . .

HE'S FULL OF GUSTO, FULL OF STEAM.
HE CHARGES UP THE WINDOW SCREEN.

AND CLINGS AND CLINGS AND CLINGS SOME MORE,
THEN . . .

SCORE!

MAX, ONE.

DOG, NONE.

DEEP INSIDE THEIR INDOOR OCEAN,
FISHES SWIM IN FISHY MOTION.

OUR KITTY BOY IS ON THE HUNT.
HE HEADS TOWARD THE OCEANFRONT.

PINK AND RED AND ORANGE, TOO.
MAX IS THINKING, FISHY STEW.

MAX'S NOSE IS TWITCHY, TWITCHY.
MAX'S TAIL IS SWITCHY, SWITCHY.

HEY, OH! . . . WHAT'S THIS?

HE LICKS HIS CHOPS; HE'S BEEN DETERRED.
IS THAT HIS FAVORITE CATNIP BIRD?

HE GRABS IT WITH HIS CATCHER CLAWS,
TOSSES IT BETWEEN HIS PAWS.

UP, UP, UP . . .

AHOY!

UH-OH—

WHERE DID THAT CATNIP BIRDIE GO?

A BASKET FILLED WITH
DIRTY SOCKS?

OH HAPPY DAY, THIS BASKET ROCKS.

HE BETTER SNAG THEM, ONE BY ONE.
HE BITES THEM ALL, AND WHEN HE'S DONE
HE FLICKS HIS EARS; HE GIVES A SCRATCH.
IT'S CLEARLY NOT AN EVEN MATCH.

SOCKS, NONE.

MAX, NINETY-ONE.

FISHES, FISHES, SWIRLS AND SWISHES;
WISHES SERVED ON KITTY DISHES . . .

SWITCHY, SWITCHY,

TWITCHY, TWITCHY . . .

HE CROUCHES LOW . . .

THEN, WHOA!

SOMETHING BOBS BENEATH THE TABLE.
CAN HE SNAG IT? IS HE ABLE?

IT'S A THING . . . A DANGLING THINGY.
NO! A STRING . . . A STRING, BY JINGIE.

THAT STRINGY SWINGS FROM SOMEONE'S SHOE.

ATTACK!

NOW MAX IS SWINGING TOO.

Arooo!

WHAT ELSE—WHAT ELSE—
CAN ONE CAT DO?

BUBBLE, BUBBLE
TWITCHY, TWITCHY

TROUBLE, TROUBLE
SWITCHY, SWITCHY

OUR SNEAKY BOY IS ON THE CREEP.
HE PEERS INTO THE OCEAN DEEP.
BACK AND FORTH THOSE FISHES GO . . .
SWISHY SWASHY, TO AND FRO.

HE PERCHES ON THAT BOWL OF WATER.

LOWER . . .

LOWER . . .

TEETER-. . .

TOTTER.

MAX'S FUR IS SLEEK AND CLEAN;
HE DRIES IT IN A SUNNY BEAM.

HE MEANT TO WASH IT ANYWAY.
HE'LL CATCH THOSE FISH ANOTHER DAY.

HIS TUMMY GROWLS. HE'S GOT THE MUNCHIES.

THERE IT IS . . . HiS BOWL OF CRUNCHIES!

OUR KITTY BOY IS TUCKERED OUT.
A BIG OL' YAWN ESCAPES HIS MOUTH.

HE CURLS UP ON HIS COZY RUG
AND GIVES HIS TRUSTY TAIL A HUG.

HE'S DONE, KAPUT, STOPPED IN HIS TRACKS.
A MIGHTY NAP ATTACKS OUR MAX.

FISHES ORANGE,
PINK,
AND RED,
SNOOZY IN
THEIR WATERBED.

THIS IS MAX.

HE ATTACKS.